D0551152

C015410425

For George with love,
Bernette

For my family,
Sam Williams

First published in Great Britain in 2012
by Boxer Books Limited
www.boxerbooks.com

Text copyright © 2012 Bernette Ford
Illustrations copyright © 2012 Sam Williams
The rights of Bernette Ford to be identified as the author and
Sam Williams as the illustrator of this work have been asserted by them
in accordance with the Copyright, Designs and Patents Act, 1988.

All rights reserved, including the right of reproduction in whole or in part in any form.
A catalogue record for this book is available from the British Library.

The illustrations were prepared using soft pencil and watercolour paint on hot press paper.
The text is set in Adobe Garamond

ISBN 978-1-907152-11-5

1 3 5 7 9 10 8 6 4 2

Printed in China

All of our papers are sourced from managed forests and renewable resources.

Ballet Kitty
Christmas Show

Bernette Ford and Sam Williams

Boxer Books

Ballet Kitty woke up feeling happy!

Christmas was only days away, and

Mademoiselle Felicity's Ballet School

was putting on a big Christmas show.

Kitty wiggled her little pink toes into
her pink leotard and tights.

Then Kitty's best friend, Princess Pussycat,

came over with a big picture book. It was

the story of The Nutcracker.

The little dancers were not going to dance

the whole ballet - just their favourite parts.

But they studied the book and listened

to the music together.

"I can't wait for ballet class," said Kitty.

"Mademoiselle will let us choose our parts

today so we can get our costumes ready."

"I already know who I'm going to be," said Pussycat. "I'm going to dance the part of the Sugar Plum Fairy.

Her costume is lilac, my favourite colour!"

"You can't be the Sugar Plum Fairy!" said Kitty.

"That's *my* favourite part.

And her costume is *not* lilac, it's pink!"

"It is not!" said Princess Pussycat. "It's lilac!"

Just then, Ginger Tom arrived to walk
to ballet class with his friends.

"Why don't you two stop arguing?" said Tom.

"You're supposed to be best friends."

Kitty and Pussycat had no more to say.

They both knew Tom was right.

At ballet school, the little dancers gathered

around Mademoiselle.

"Has everyone chosen a part?" she asked.

"I'm the Nutcracker!" said Tom.

"I'm the Sugar Plum Fairy!" said Kitty
and Pussycat together.

"You can't both be the Sugar Plum Fairy,"
said Mademoiselle. "Wouldn't one of you
like to be a Snowflake?"

That night in bed, a big tear rolled
down Ballet Kitty's face. Princess Pussycat
was her very best friend. She didn't want
to be angry at her.

In her bed, Princess Pussycat sniffled.

"I want to be the Sugar Plum Fairy," she said.

"But such a silly little thing should not keep me

from talking to my best friend."

A few days later, Ballet Kitty woke up happy.

She jumped out of bed and did a pirouette.

Kitty had had a great idea.

Princess Pussycat woke up feeling happy, too.

Tonight was the big Christmas show,

and Pussycat had had a great idea.

That night at ballet school, Ginger Tom

looked great as the Nutcracker.

When Princess Pussycat arrived, she was

wearing a lovely Snowflake costume!

Then in came Ballet Kitty, dressed as

a beautiful Snowflake too!

The three little dancers jumped up and down

as they gave each other a big group hug.

Later, Kitty and Pussycat stood in the wings

and watched Ginger Tom on stage.

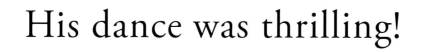

His dance was thrilling!

Even Mademoiselle

was smiling.

Then the girls floated on to the stage in their beautiful costumes. They heard the tinkling piano begin to play "The Waltz of the Snowflakes."

They pointed their toes.

They stretched
out their arms.

They bent and swayed
with the music.

The whole audience clapped and cheered.

The Christmas show was a big success!

After the show, the three friends walked

arm in arm together. It had begun to snow.

They were going to Ballet Kitty's house

for a Christmas party. It was too soon

for such a lovely night to end!